USBORNE BIBLE TALES

DANIEL AND THE LIONS

Retold by Heather Amery

Illustrated by Norman Young
Designed by Maria Wheatley

Language consultant: Betty Root
Series editor: Jenny Tyler

This is Daniel.

He lived a long time ago in Jerusalem. When he was young, the city was captured by an enemy army.

Daniel was taken to Babylon.

He lived with other boys. They had good food and went to school. Daniel prayed to God every day.

Daniel grew up very wise.

He lived at the King's palace. He was very good at telling people what their dreams meant.

He was made a ruler.

He was put in charge of two other rulers and many princes. They ruled the country for the King.

The two rulers hated Daniel.

They wanted to get rid of him. They tried to find something he had done wrong but Daniel was good.

The two rulers went to the King.

"King Darius," they said, "make a law that everyone must pray only to you or they must die."

Daniel heard about the law.

He would not obey it. He knelt by his window three times every day and prayed to God.

The two rulers watched him.

They hid among the trees. Then they went off to tell the King about Daniel.

The King was very sad.

He liked and trusted Daniel. But he had made a law and Daniel had broken it. Daniel must die.

Daniel was arrested.

He was put into a pit full of hungry lions. “May your God protect you,” the King shouted to Daniel.

The King went to his palace.

He was so upset, he didn't want anything to eat and he couldn't sleep. He sent his servants away.

The King went to the lion pit.

It was very early the next morning. “Daniel, did your God save you?” he shouted down into the pit.

"I'm here, Oh King."

"God sent his angel to stop the lions from killing me," said Daniel. "God knows I've done no wrong."

The King was delighted.

He had Daniel set free. Then he told his guards to put the two rulers and the princes into the pit.

The King made a new law.

He ordered everyone in his kingdom to pray to Daniel's God. God had saved Daniel from the lions.

This edition first published in 2004 by Usborne Publishing Ltd, 83-85 Saffron Hill, London EC1N 8RT, England. www.usborne.com UE. This edition first published in America in 2004. Printed in Belgium.